An Evening of Enigma

Naisha

Ukiyoto Publishing

All global publishing rights are held by

Ukiyoto Publishing

Published in 2022

Content Copyright © **Naisha**

Edited by **Priyanga Soundar**

ISBN 9789360163655

*All rights reserved.
No part of this publication may be reproduced, transmitted, or stored in a retrieval system, in any form by any means, electronic, mechanical, photocopying, recording, or otherwise, without the prior permission of the publisher.*

The moral rights of the author have been asserted.

This is a work of fiction. Names, characters, businesses, places, events, locales, and incidents are either the products of the author's imagination or used in a fictitious manner. Any resemblance to actual persons, living or dead, or actual events is purely coincidental.

This book is sold subject to the condition that it shall not by way of trade or otherwise, be lent, resold, hired out, or otherwise circulated, without the publisher's prior consent, in any form of binding or cover other than that in which it is published.

*This title is produced in Association with
Pachyderm Tales*

www.pachydermtales.com

> "The universe is a place full of mysteries."

Yes, the curiosity of learning about the universe opens up a lot of unknown mysteries. Well, this was the first thing I heard this morning in my dream. I felt something was different today when I woke up. Something that made me excited and kindled my curiosity.

Oops!

I forgot to introduce myself, I am Naisha.

I am curious, creative and sometimes a little bit messy.

Oh no! That is a different case but it's time and I need to get ready for school or I will be late. I for sure do not want to be punished.

An Evening of Enigma

My Mom shouted, "Naisha get ready soon or you will be late for school!"

"Aaah! Yes mom, I'm getting ready," I replied.

I was running late.

"But where is my shirt that I pressed last night?

Got it, never mind." I cheered myself.

I had to hurry!

"Mom I am dressed up. Could you give me my glass of milk?"

"Yes, sure! Here you go and do not forget to get your science project with you," said my mom.

I got my daily glass of milk that I drink in the morning and took my science project too.

"Oh, thank you for the reminder, I nearly forgot that. The milk was very tasty too." I responded to mom!

It was then I heard the loud honk of my school bus waiting for me, outside my home.

"Oh! The bus is here. Bye, mom! See you after school." I rushed out to get my school bus.

An Evening of Enigma

I got on the bus and headed towards my school.

"Phew! Got here just on time."

***

The first period was about to begin.

"Hi Monika, how are you?"

"I am fine thank you Naisha. Hey! Are you excited about the group activity that we have today? Did you bring your project?" asked Monika.

"Yes, I am super excited. Astronomy is one of my favourite subjects and I enjoy it, I am very curious to learn new things and it feels like I am connected to the vast space. I often feel that planets, moons and stars talk to me…

An Evening of Enigma

When I look up in the sky,

I wish that I could be a rocket and soar so high!

I go far to space,

To the moons and to the stars, that I face.

I feel so excited and magical,

For this vast space and I am so fanatical.

I wish to live in my dream,

Travelling so fast like a light beam,

In excitement, I loudly scream.

I recited this poem of mine to Monica and she liked it very much.

Monica had been my best friend since the day when I joined this school.

We always stay together and travel together on this roller coaster ride called 'life'.

We always have each other's back and support each other.

We care for each other like sisters!

"Oh! The teacher is here.

Good morning Teacher!"

The teacher greeted us back and she brought a new student to our class

"Students, we have a new student! She will be joining us from today! Meet Sophie."

"Hello, Sophie!" We all greeted Sophie, the new student.

"Naisha! Let Sophie join in your group for the group discussion," instructed our teacher.

We were happy to join Sophie in our group.

"Sophie you can join our group. I am Naisha and she is Monika. We can be good friends,"

and this is how we got introduced.

***

Well, let me tell you the first impression I got seeing Sophie for the first time.

I noticed that her eyes were beautiful, green in colour just like a green lake or a green emerald. She had curly hair like the sea waves and was wearing a beautiful necklace with a flower on it!

As the day continued we had our mathematics class, science class, astronomy class and so on.

Sophie was not too good in maths but was outstanding in science and astronomy just like me.

I was quite impressed with her. She was extremely friendly and kind. We both had a lot in common and instantly became friends.

Her voice was so soft and she was also intelligent.

She said, she was much interested in knowing more about space and celestial bodies just like me. I thought this might be very useful for our project.

Sophie, Monica and I worked together on our project titled,

'Can life sustain on planets other than earth?'

We were having a hard time preparing for our project.

We were unable to find solid facts and evidences.

We did some research but could not find anything.

Then Sophie broke the silence and started telling us about 'Greenophasia' a planet where life can sustain itself.

We were shocked and could not believe what she said.

It seemed impossible, so we decided to check on it and did some research.

Later it turned out to be a fact. We were jaw-dropped!

"How did we not know this?" we questioned ourselves.

It was a huge discovery and a huge help to our project. I was left spellbound knowing there can be life on other planets too, which means aliens are real! This changed my whole perception of space.

We were prepared to present our project, we spoke one at a time.

Now it was Sophie's turn and Oh my!

Let me tell you, she had a lot of knowledge about the topic more than us. She was very well equipped with the facts, proofs and evidences.

She said "the universe is still unexplored and there are so many planets just like Earth which could sustain life," this became my favourite part of our project.

She continued and said so many fascinating facts about the planet

'GREENOPHASIA'

This tingled my senses and reminded me of my dream. It got a feel that universe was conveying something to me but I could not simply comprehend the message.

The message was important and deep but what was it? I continued and ignored it anyway.

Sophie was a confident speaker and left everyone in the class amazed. Everyone was impressed by the way she presented.

The way she narrated made me feel like an astronaut, exploring space. I dived right into my world of imagination, imagining meeting an alien from Greenophasia. Then when reality struck back, I thought it would have been so cool if it happened. The teacher liked our presentation and we won the 1st prize.

Then we were called on the stage and I had butterflies in my stomach but still felt happy about the project we made.

Sophie was also excited as this was her first day and she had already made new friends and got selected for the presentation that we enjoyed a lot.

Later, we were called by the Principal after the classes. She asked us to further prepare points for the presentation for we had to present it to a higher-level of audience this time. My heart was pounding and it almost skipped a beat. I was overjoyed by the news that I received from my principal.

We had to practice for our presentation so at the end of the day. Sophie asked us to come over to her home to discuss our project.

I was thrilled to visit her home for the very first time.

An Evening of Enigma

We both got ready and went to her home the next day.

Her home was a little far away from ours, so Monica's dad drove us there. Soon we reached her home and everyone at her home looked as kind as she is. Her parents were really sweet and treated us well. Her home was stunning it gave us a sci-fi futuristic feel. There were many beautiful paintings of galaxies and space on the walls. Then my eyes saw something unexpected that I had never noticed before. Sophie had a tattoo! And not only Sophie but her whole family had the same tattoo.

Though having a tattoo was not such a big deal but it triggered something in me and it made me more curious.

I felt something was odd about it. I ignored it and thought the day is just weird.

I observed that all were having weird tattoos on their hand. Not exactly weird but something unique and it was also so beautiful.

The tattoo was green in colour and had golden glittering leaves inside a circle. I was thinking that it could be a family symbol.

I had so many questions and mixed thoughts about that tattoo and it looked much strange when I looked at it again and again but anyways we all had a project to make so we got into our business.

We worked hard on our project by doing more research but we were unable to discover more information about the topic.

Sophie cheered us by saying, "it's alright, we are just tired so let's take a break and have some snacks. My mom makes delicious snacks."

How could we deny it? So we went to wash our hands and we were ready to have a snack feast.

And when we returned, hot delicious snacks were already there on our table, waiting for us. I am not exaggerating but Sophie's mom made delicious snacks. The food was remarkable and we all relished it till we filled our tummies.

After we were done eating our snack feast, we went to wash our hands and noticed that Monica had left the tap open and the water was getting wasted this whole time.

I was concerned and insisted her not to do it again but Sophie was just so angry and so upset they both started an argument.

We didn't know early that, Sophie a sweet, kind girl could get so much anger. Monica was left speechless by her unseen behaviour of Sophie. She was just as confused as I was. With Sophie's sudden anger, Monica lost her temper too. She felt sorry for her mistake and said she didn't mean to do it on purpose.

Sophie yelled loudly and accentuated that every drop you wasted could have saved a life.

Sophie's mom heard the commotion and came to our room. She tried to explain to Sophie but she didn't listen and she was reacting much and it was not much water that was let out wasted.

Then suddenly she stopped quarrelling after her mom told her something. It was like her mother was trying to tell something through her facial expressions and then she finally calmed down.

"Thank god!" I exclaimed.

"Buzzzzzz buzz"

Monica's phone rang.

She went outside to attend the call. She was super happy after attending that phone call and she told us that her father was a building contractor and they cleared 500 acres of forests and made a profitable contract for making Malls, Airports and many other buildings.

"It is great news for our family!" She exclaimed with joy.

Before I could react or say anything to Monica, Sophie just burst out crying, shedding tears. Her tears were flowing down like a river. Her tears were getting trapped in her curly hair, her eyes turned red, and her face showed anger like she had exploded from some sort of confinement of emotions that she was holding for so long. It looked like she was holding up secrets from us for a long time that came out as tears. We were so confused over the sudden reaction of Sophie.

"What was there to cry so hard Sophie?" We asked her repeatedly.

Monica was annoyed as it was good news for her family and she was crying like someone had passed away. We thought Sophie went crazy.

Sophie's mom came into our room hearing Sophie cry out loud. This time Sophie's mom couldn't handle it and told us that she had gone through a lot in life. Remember the weird tattoo I told you about? It started glowing and Sophie started floating in midair and we were shocked and also scared.

With aggression she said,

"All human beings are selfish. Do you guys even care about the earth? I am going to tell you guys the truth. I am an alien from the planet Greenophasia and I was just like you, wasting water and misusing the available natural resources, taking everything for granted as if it is going to last forever. But one day our planet ran out of resources and food was scarce. People were thirsty, people were dying and no one was there to quench our thirst and hunger. We were searching for the last grain that would be enough for a day or even for a month. The air, the water, the food, our nature everything was condemned. We lost our loved ones and no technology could save us. We were fighting for our withering life!"

Hearing all these words from Sophie made me feel sad and I started imagining our earth in the place of Greenophasia. Sophie continued as I was thinking of this.

"I even lost my little sister who died out of hunger and thirst. I can never forgive myself for every drop I wasted, she could have been alive if I had only saved the natural resources. This necklace is all I have as her last remembrance and I always wear it this remembering her. When you left the tap open, memories of my sister dying out of thirst and hunger rewinded in my mind which triggered my anger and rage. I can never forget the tragedy."

Sophie got emotional while talking about her sister and the memories they had together. And how she misses her dear sister.

"My father was a rocket scientist and somehow we managed to escape, realising that we were the only survivor in our planet. My life completely changed after that incident we had to adjust on earth and act like humans and start a whole new journey," Said Sophie.

After Sophie told her story we were shocked and full of guilt Monica started crying and said,

"Now I understood why it is a great concern to you when I left the tap open and told you about my father's occupation. I am so sorry."

Sophie in turn asked us not to reveal the truth about her and her family and also she asked us to conserve and use the available natural resources without wasting them. We both promised her that we would do whatever she asks and we also decided to create awareness among other classmates in our school and protect nature. Yes, indeed the universe is a mysterious place, we all are lucky to have everything satisfying our needs and we should be grateful for what we have instead of demanding more and thus ruining what we have. Make sure that you learn this lesson and decide to protect mother nature or you might need an alien friend to open your eyes and show you the bitter truth.

"The greatest threat to our planet is the belief that someone else will save it."

The Author

Naisha is a 13-year-old girl. She has an interest in literature and loves to write stories and poems. Like all other kids, Naisha loves to play and participate in co-curricular activities in school. Her interests in creative writing and literature make her unique from the kids of her age.

HETS is an Education Consulting and Service Company exclusively dealing with end-to-end Education service provider Pan India. Our team works with our educational Institutions in planning, developing, and managing educational institutions that meet their vision, mission, and goals. HETS has more than a decade of experience setting up and running schools and pre-schools across the country.

HETS aims to impart education beyond books, wherein Educators should create relevant Learning amidst the accelerating change of the environment to grow in a climate of non-threatening, respect, and trust where teachers need to be empowered rightly to create innovators and researchers in them for the right teaching and technology-driven. To bring in a change and transform the lives of students, Empower women, and upliftment of society with passion and dedication.

Harvest Educational Transformation Solution is a single point of contact for Institutions, organizations, and individuals customized based on Training and mentoring. HETS engages an evolutionary change in the education sector by implementing academics and sharing knowledge and experience to create a change in the education sector with multiple accessibilities to resources.

Dr. Aruna Wadkar is currently the Founder and Managing Director at Harvest Educational Transformation Solutions registered with MSME, Government of India, ISO 9001-2015 certified, an organization which has turned out to be her dream project, and her dream venture took another progressive turn with the Launch of HETS Pratishtha India - NGO Foundation in 2021 where she aspires to empower women, children, and people across all genders, academic drop outs through education, knowledge, skill development, training and improving employability scope through Educational and Corporate training.

www.ingramcontent.com/pod-product-compliance
Lightning Source LLC
LaVergne TN
LVHW041600070526
838199LV00046B/2068